CW01619039

Tears to Joy

BlueRose Publishers

© Mary Gladys Pavamani 2020

All rights reserved

All rights reserved by author. No part of this publication may be reproduced, stored in a retrieval system or transmitted in any form or by any means, electronic, mechanical, photocopying, recording or otherwise, without the prior permission of the author.

Although every precaution has been taken to verify the accuracy of the information contained herein, the author and publisher assume no responsibility for any errors or omissions. No liability is assumed for damages that may result from the use of information contained within.

First Published in April 2020

ISBN: 978-81-945232-2-2

BLUE ROSE PUBLISHERS
www.bluerosepublishers.com
info@bluerosepublishers.com
+91 8882 898 898

Cover Design:
Tyngshain Pariat

Typographic Design:
Teena Maurya

Distributed by: Blue Rose, Amazon, Flipkart, Shopclues

Contents

Tears To Joy

I'm Holding All

I'm holding all,
This early morn.
The song of the bird,
The small waterfall,
The breeze,
The fisherman crying out loud,
The cars horn.
I'm holding all.

I'm holding all.
Your heart beating,
The pulse in your feet,
My breath surging,
All through you,
I'm holding all.

I'm holding all.
Your loves and your joys, your smiles,

More so your pain,

Your sorrows, your sighs, your tears.

I'm holding all.

Your worries, your anxieties,

All your thoughts, your emotions.

All you have

From top to toe

I need it all.

For every moment, I'm weaving a brand new world

For you and for Me.

I'm holding all.

I need to churn something new

Out of all you are and have

Out of what you loved and lost,

To this heartless world.

I want to create something great and new

Out of this godforsaken rubble.

I'm just holding all.

Yes, I'm watching and waiting

For the emerging world.

My Coppersmith Barbet

It was this same coppersmith barbet
That once led me to school.
She was my dear mother
This bird.

Too small,
I always lagged behind
But she hopped from tree to tree, singing.
Leading me to school
Leaving me there
Till I came back.

Now here she is, once more
All the way from Cuttack to Calicut
From my 1965 to my now
Just outside my window!
Still singing to me!

'Yes, it was because of you dear barbet
I've reached this moment in time
Thaaank you, Mother!'
O! She's just the same
My sweet coppersmith barbet
But I've grown so old.

This Whiff of Love

This whiff of love
Wafted in by a tiny leaf
When the breeze brushed it in.
Directly it fell on my lap.
I took it in fully
The perfumes still lingering.
It fills my whole being.
I turn into a dewdrop
Not wanting to dry.
A blue mist
Not wanting to rain.
A fresh breath of cool vapour,
Not wanting to exhale.
In short, I'm mummified,
Not wanting to let go
I preserve myself intact.

O! This world of Mine!

O! This world of mine!
All small with small dreams!
Small contraptions
Made with tiny twigs
To keep things in place.
There's a semblance of great control
But nothing works for long
This way or that.
It doesn't last.
Just silly thoughts and feelings!
That all is well and will go well.
It's only for a moment.
That things seem to stand in place
Or seem to.
And then comes the break
And the whole thing flops.
And all lies crumbled
Like pie crust on the carpet!

Amma

I've gotten over Amma
And it is sad.

There was a time
When I was her tail
Running behind her zig-zag.
In and out of rooms
She either in front or at the back, always
Till I slept.

But now.
To think of it now
It's years since she's elsewhere
And totally out of my sight.
Now I fold my feelings into covers
And send it by post.

The blood has just dried
At the roots.

A Funny Wedding

We went to this wedding
Just the both of us
There was no one else.
Only you and me.

There was no bride
And there was no groom.
Only you and me.

There was no cake
And there was no wine.
Only you and me.

There were no flowers
And there were no lights.
Only you and me.

There was no song
And there was no dance.
Only you and me.

There were no guests
And there was no food.
Only you and me.

We went to this wedding.
Just the both of us.
There was no one else.
There was nothing else.

Only you and me.

Oh! My God!
Really funny!
Really funny!
This wedding!

Fading Away

If it's a leaf
It buds, pushes out, blooms,
And then dies away.
Look at the sun
It rises in the east and sets in the west.

Everything here has a season.

Our seasons too,
Rise like the sun
And bud like the leaves.
Our twilights may try their best
To stop the coming darkness.
And our suns may hate the thought
Of rising elsewhere.
But Love dies.
For Eternity lies elsewhere.

My Space

I'm not a beggar
That's why I left you.
If I had not left you,
I'd still be begging you
For the each morsel of life we shared.
And would have been left
Tattered and torn in a hut
Dark and all alone.

That's why I left you.

My mind sees a waterfall.
Or a huge harvest.
A whole sea
Or great garners.
Oh my God!
I'm not used to drops.
Or rations.
Or measures.

That's why I left you.
It's impossible to live in your small mean world.

A Mother's Song

I love birds
Because I do not have
Wings to fly
Just into the sky
Or another world.

I love cats
Because I do not have
Their glazed eyes
Staring into outer space.

The squirrels I see
Brown furry things
Hurry to some remote heaven
I can never reach.

The fish
Blue, red, and green
I can never have
The peace they feel.

I love my daughter
Because I do not have
Her tiny body and soul
So beautiful!

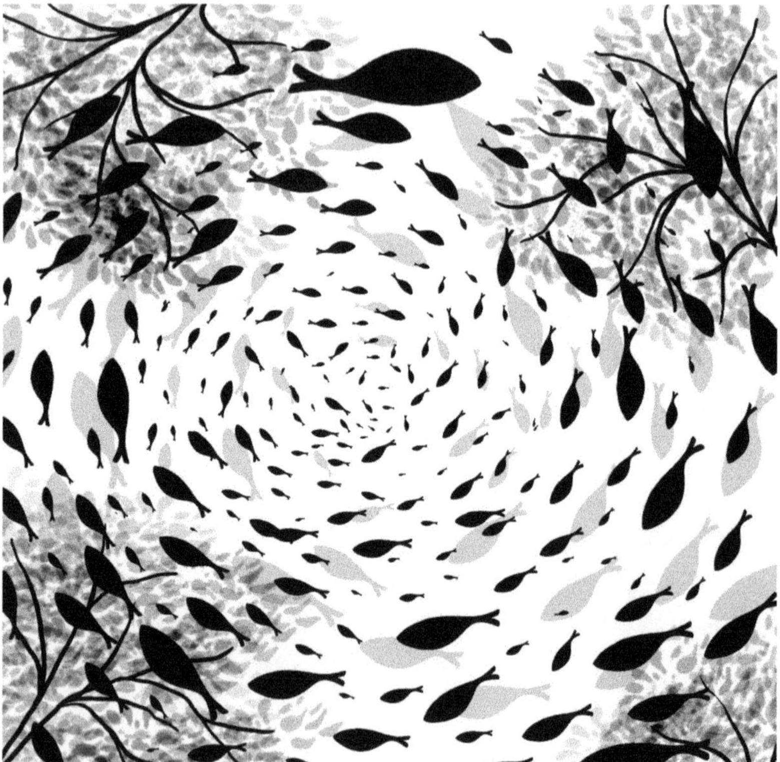

A Million Thoughts

A million thoughts rush to you

Each moment.

Its like an endless shoal in the sea

Surely, I can live without you!

I Am That I Am

I am that I am,
In the tiniest of tiny flowers,
All blue,
That blooms in your garden
Under the stones,
With the sun kissing it.

Wrapped in My silence,
They bask in My glory.

The world comes and goes,
Not seeing them,
Not knowing them,
But it matters little to Me.

I look upon the world

Through the tiniest of tiny flowers,

All blue,

That blooms in your garden

Under the stones,

With the sun kissing it.

The world moves on

Not seeing Me.

Not knowing Me.

Wrapped in their troubles and their traumas,

Lost in their egos.

If only they looked upon Me

I could completely heal them

And change them into blue flowers

That bloom in your garden under the stones,

With the sun kissing it.

My Dear Cricket!

Chatterbox!

Chattering away in the dark

Just outside my window

Non-stop and loud,

Trying to get my attention

To talk back to her.

But I couldn't see her or get to know her

Even just to say a hello

Before the train moved on.

I strained my head through the window bars

Sorry, I couldn't get a glimpse of this cosmic friend of mine

Who flashed into my presence for a moment,

Trying to get my attention

And then gone.

Gone forever.

This tiny miraculous friend of mine,

Who flooded the world with her presence,

It's a tragedy

I could not take in her loving aura

Even for a moment.

But the train moved on.

And once more, I was pushed into the brash noise of the world

Missing the moments of heaven with this cricket friend of mine.

Which I lost.

My dear Cricket

Maybe we'll catch up somewhere in eternity.

Please accept my silent goodbye!

MALABAR CHRISTIAN
COLLEGE

For Malabar Christian College

O! My dear Worlds!

Torpedoed in a second!

And then, each time I find myself

Rummaging through the debris

To collect a memory or two

To keep forever.

And as I speed on

I see my dear Christian College too

On the brink of such a collapse!

O! Lord! Help me hold on to this sweet world of mine

For a little while longer.

Searching for You

Where is the dawn, Lord?
Have You overlaid it with the sand?
Where is the flower?
Have You camouflaged it in the bramble?
Where is the dewdrop?
Is it embalmed in the desert?
The tiny ray of light?
You've shrouded it in the darkness?

I'm working it out.
Searching.
Searching ceaselessly
For a hint of You
For a tiny trace of Your Light in the dewdrop
For the delicate scent of Your presence in the petal.
I'm looking out.
Straining my eyes, nose and ears for You.
Where, Lord, have You hid them?
Hid Yourself?

My Baby

Years ago when I joined here
You were just a tiny tree,
Silently standing outside my class,
Waving to me.

Daily I saw you
Dearly I loved you
Like the baby I had at home.

Now, twenty years have passed.

And here I am, still taking my class
While you silently stand outside
All grown and strong and sturdy!

I just love you, dear tree
For being there for me
So close and not going away.
'Cause I don't know what happened to my baby.

All My Friends for Gone Forever

I had a hundred friends
Now all have dwindled one-by-one
And all are gone forever.

The many hands that carried me and held me tight
The hands that clothed me and fed me
Now those hands are gone forever.

I remember the fair hands with blue veins
That bathed me in hot water
I remember the ruby ring on its fingers
But now it's gone forever!

I remember the gnarled hands
That wiped away the sweat on my body
All throughout the dark night when I fell sick
But now it's gone forever.

I remember the powerful hands that lifted me up
And made me hold the star sparkles
But now those hands are gone forever.

So many smiles,
So many breaths,
So many kisses,
So many heartbeats,
All so near to me,
Just next to my face,
So full of love...
But now they are all gone forever.

A hundred friends
One here , one there, and all around me.
A woven lace network of love
That held me .
Now the holes gape at me
One by one they have dwindled
And their lights gone off.

And here I sit in front of my roses
White, pink, red and yellow
Thinking of my friends who are gone forever.
But their love inhabits my being
And I am rich because of their many colours
Though they have gone forever.

Hero worship

I like the way you look at me,
Without looking at me
The way you get me reflected to the wall in front,
Or someone else.

I like the way you smile at me
Without smiling at me
The way you smile when I'm around
At someone you just don't know.

I like the way you talk to me
Without talking to me.
The way you talk to my friend
And get me to talk to you through her.

I like this odd relationship of ours,
There's a funny novelty in it
I want to keep it this way,
This odd way of getting to know each other.

My Garden Angel

Oh! My soft white angel!

The way you held me for a whole minute!

Right from the tip of my nose

To the pores

On the tips of my toes

To engulf my whole body

With your fragrant embrace.

So much so that I wished to God

The rest of my breaths

May so be perfumed.

Wonderstruck

There's not much time left
For you and me here on earth.

So I sit in obeisance
In front of you tiny leaf!
To examine your minute veins.

To follow with my eyes
In prayerful wonder
The patterns on your wings, dear butterfly!

To stand spell-bound and watch
Your endless string ant army!
Carrying your sugar grains.

There's not much time left
For you and me here on earth
To live through
The glorious fission
Of His creation.

Frozen Fossil

Today I had a chilling experience
With your eyes
Piercing me like pointed pieces of ice
I got frozen for a while,
Unable to take them out
Or melt them with my smile.

I wish you were the Sun
And me a dot of sand
Then you could turn me into a diamond
And not a fossil instead.

Hibernation

The cavern is too deep
Almost touching the earth's core.
And there lies buried
My poor Familiar.
Dust heaped on dust
Upon my poor Angel.
Can you rise up, once more,
Like Vesuvius to rescue me
Or have you decided to
Hibernate for centuries.

This Small Strand of Hair

This small strand of hair
Just denies to live
And chooses to be grey,
Adamantly.
Not minding the consequences of being white,
Admidst the rest of the luxurious black.

Today she jumped out
Like a spike
Right on my hair line,
As if reminding me of
The world's cruelty.

And then I saw
How every part in me too
Just denies to live
And chooses to be grey,
Adamantly.
Not minding the consequences of being white
To remind the world
Of your cruelty.

The Rain Falls in Drizzles

The rain falls in drizzles

Like my thoughts

Drizzling about you.

Won't the rain stop?

I hate this drizzle.

Death Round the Corner

There was death in every smile
But I did not know.
There was death in every glance
But I did not know.
There was death in every step
But I did not know.
For years together,
Death was round the corner
But I did not know.

All through the years
Someone stepped in each time
And I stepped out.
But I did not know.

And so it is, even now,
When there is death in a smile,
In a step,
Or a look.
This Someone steps in
And I step out
To move on.
This is Salvation.
And you know what I mean.

Please Pull Me Out of This Tsunami.

Can You hold me tight
And breathe life into me?
Hold my hand in a tight grip
And pull me out of this Tsunami?

Can You make some clay with Your spittle
And open my eyes?
And take me to Your new world?
I'm just waiting for Your word
To drop my grave clothes.
To jump up from my seat
And get into the rippling pool!

Are You my Christ?
Can I believe
That You are Him
To save me.

Paws

I cannot be without paws in my house.
Paws walking softly through the rooms
Or flitting across.
Sometimes coming out with claws
At my legs, scratching,
Or pressing warm pads on my lap
To settle down for a nap.

I've got these paws now at home,
Small pink paws
No bigger than flower-buds
But naughty with claws.
That sends my mother screeching
And all the rest cursing.
But I can't do without this
Ball of fur
At my legs or on my lap,
Living it up.

My Goddess Pet

You're so enshrined in my mind.
Every now and then, I find myself
Smile and gaze at you dearly.
You keep endlessly wondering about
The where, the which, and the why
Of your existence in my life.

I'm confused!
For I don't believe in past births.

Just like it keeps me endlessly wondering
About the way he smiles with his eyes
Whenever he sees me.

The Friendly Cheat

Money, you are the biggest deceiver I've ever known,
No sooner have I taken you out,
You're sharing another's hand.
How you roll on the counter, you glamourous creature,
And so politely disappear.

I've read somewhere
There's no reason whatsoever
To like one person and dislike another
Do you too have this human nature?
Or else, why the rich richer, and the poor poorer?

Indeed you've great magic
Or else, how, though so ancient and historic
You still remain man's favorite topic
In spite of all his powers of yoga and logic,
The situation still remains really tragic,
Or do you find all this comic?

There's a Song in My Heart

It has no rhythm or rhyme,
Neither any notes .
It's not of this world.

With this, my song,
The world suddenly turns beautiful
The little bird's breast yellower
The jasmine more white.

With this, my song,
The world gets so glittery
It sparkles like a bubble.
I wish I could hold her
In the palm of my hand forever.

Wow! This, my song,
May it never end.
May it go on forever.

My Rainbow to You

I'm rainbowed with Your blessings
I sense the buds pushing out to flower.
To glorify You.
I wait with all my hope.
For the whole thing to bud up.
I see a whole new world
Coming on to embrace me.

Dear Mother

No more can I come
To greet you at your door in the morning
And eat the soft bread and milk
That you keep ready for me daily.

No more can I run to the small red potty
That I jump into
Only my head sticking out
The sight you loved so much.

No more can I sit on your lap
With my small body and dose off to sleep.

No more the nice things with you, mother
No more your heaven for me.

Last night
A silly dog bit me
And I was forced to leave for outer space.
But I'm right here,
In a small corner of your mind
'cause I don't need much space.

So long, dear mother,
Till we meet again,
I'll always be the tiny cat you loved so much

Dark venom

The face was fair.
But under the skin
One could see the slow undercurrent of dark venom.
There was a sudden sharp look
And a thousand fangs came hissing out.
Poison through each pore
Was spewing at me.

But Your light
Burnt the whole thing up.
The scorched evil rose up like black carbon
And vanished in a moment.
Its tail slithering off silently around the corner
And there I stood untouched
Smiling.

www.ingramcontent.com/pod-product-compliance
Ingram Content Group UK Ltd.
Pitfield, Milton Keynes, MK11 3LW, UK
UKHW041626291225
9789UKWH00037B/1115

9 788194 523222